LITTLE GREEN PUMPKINS

Story and Pictures by Christa Chevalier

ALBERT WHITMAN & COMPANY, CHICAGO

For Schwanz, which is short for Dave

Library of Congress Cataloging in Publication Data

Chevalier, Christa.
    Little green pumpkins.

    Summary: Spence plants a gourd seed and expects
it to grow little pumpkins.
    [1. Gourds—Fiction.   2. Gardening—Fiction]
I. Title.
PZ7.C42557Li   [E]   81-12999
ISBN 0-8075-4593-7   AACR2

The text of this book is set in eighteen point Fairfield.

110081

Spence,
which is short for Spencer,
found a gourd.
It was an old gourd.

When Spence squeezed the gourd, it crumbled.

Inside,
Spence found lots of little seeds.

When he showed the seeds to his mother,
she said, "Why don't you put
one of those seeds in some soil?"

"Why?" asked Spence.

"Because," said his mother,
"it will grow into a plant."

"My very own?" asked Spence.

"Your very own," said his mother.

"Will my plant grow and grow?" asked Spence.

"I'm sure," said his mother.

"And when it is all grown,
I will have a big pumpkin,"
said Spence.

"No, Spence," said his mother.
"You will have lots of little gourds."

"Why?" asked Spence.

"Because," said his mother,

"your little seed came from a gourd."

"Oh!" said Spence.

Spence's mother showed him
how to plant his seed,

how to water his seed.

She showed him where to set it
on the windowsill
so the sun could warm it.

Spence checked his seed every day.

"Nothing yet?" asked his mother.
"Nothing yet," said Spence.
"Don't worry," said his mother.
"It will grow. You'll see."

And one day it did.

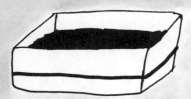 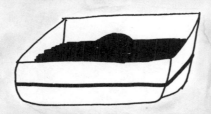 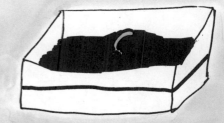

Spence looked at his plant.
"It's so small," he said.
"Of course!" said his mother.
"Why?" asked Spence.
"A plant is like a person," said his mother.
"It starts out very small."

When Spence's plant had two leaves, he asked, "Is it finished yet?"

"No," said his mother.
"Why not?" asked Spence.
"Because growing takes time," said his mother.

"How long does it take to grow a pumpkin?"
asked Spence.

"A long time," said his mother.
"And the seed won't grow a pumpkin,
remember? It will grow lots of little gourds."

When the plant had four leaves,
Spence's mother showed him how to plant it in the garden.
"Now it can really grow," said Spence.

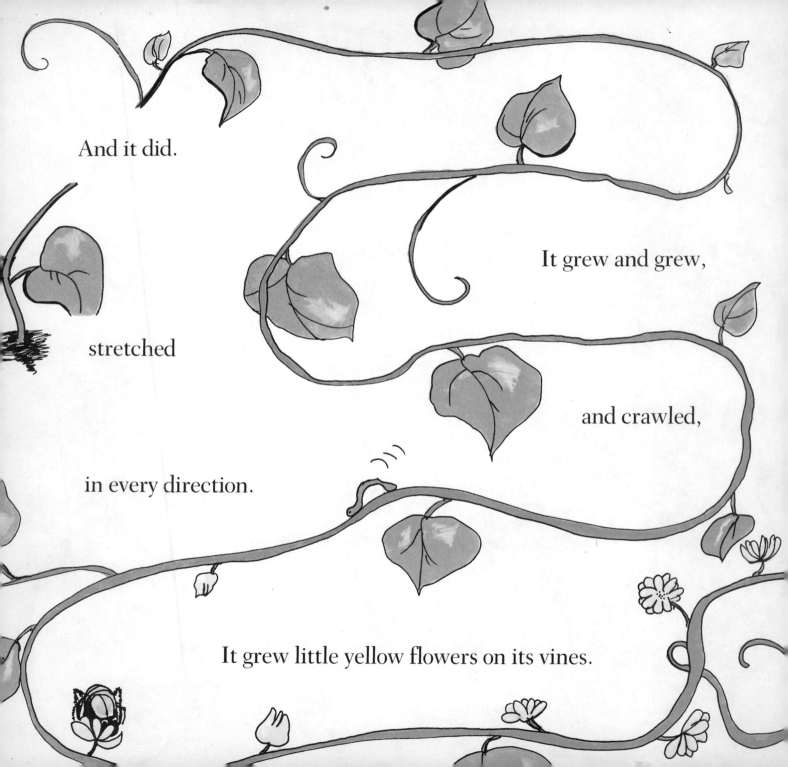

And it did.

It grew and grew,

stretched

and crawled,

in every direction.

It grew little yellow flowers on its vines.

And when the flowers fell off,
it grew little green berries.

Spence looked at the berries.
"My plant is growing little green pumpkins,"
he said.

"Gourds," said his mother.
"It's growing little green gourds."

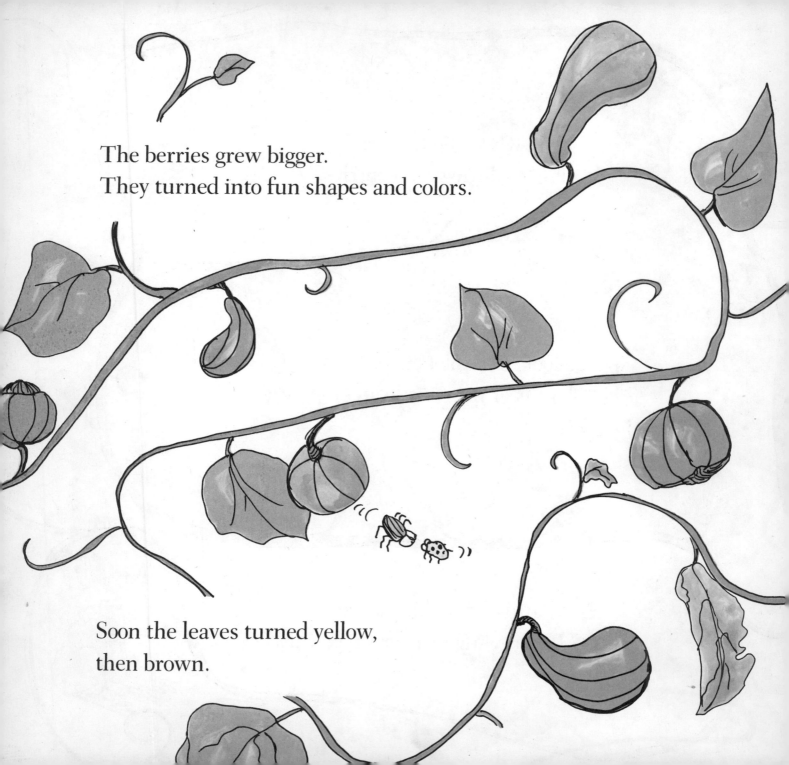

The berries grew bigger.
They turned into fun shapes and colors.

Soon the leaves turned yellow,
then brown.

"Is it finished?" asked Spence.

"It is finished," said his mother.

Spence picked all the fun-shaped things off the vines.
He spread them out on the ground.
"Here," he said,
and handed one to his mother.
"You can have one of my pumpkins."

"Oh, Spence!" said his mother.
Then she smiled.
"I fooled you," said Spence,
and he giggled.
"I knew they were gourds all the time."

Christa Chevalier was born in Germany and studied
art in Braunschweig and Wiesbaden. She has
taught art to adults and book designing to children.

Christa loves gardening, cooking, reading, skiing,
and collecting old-time stuff. She lives most
contentedly with her husband and their dog
in an old house in Richford, a small community
in northern Vermont.

DATE DUE

FE 18 '88	SE 21 '93		
MR 11 '88	NO 09 '93		
JY 14 '88	SE 09 '94		
JY 29 '88	OC 05 '94		
NO 08 '88	OC 13 '94		
NO 21 '88	NO 16 '94		
FE 20 '89	SE 05 '95		
MR 08 '89	NO 24 '97		
AP 07 '89	MR 27 '00		
JY 09 '90	DEC 21 '00		
OC 31 '90	SE 20 '01		
JA 17 '91	SEP 29		
MR 07 '91			
MY 04 '91			
OC 28 '92			
AP 06 '93			
JY 28 '93			